SOLANO COUNTY LIBRARY

JAN   1995   VACAVILLE

D0535720

SOLANO COUNTY LIBRARY

214

WHEN THE FLY FLEW IN...

by Lisa Westberg Peters

pictures by Brad Sneed

Dial Books for Young Readers

NEW YORK

Published by Dial Books for Young Readers
A Division of Penguin Books USA Inc.
375 Hudson Street
New York, New York 10014
Text copyright © 1994 by Lisa Westberg Peters
Pictures copyright © 1994 by Brad Sneed
All rights reserved
Design by Jane Byers Bierhorst
Printed in Hong Kong by South China
Printing Company (1988) Limited
First Edition
1 2 3 4 5 6 7 8 9 10

Library of Congress Cataloging in Publication Data

Peters, Lisa Westberg
When the fly flew in...
by Lisa Westberg Peters ; pictures by Brad Sneed
p. cm.
Summary: Although a young child puts off cleaning the
bedroom because all the family's pets are asleep there, the
sudden arrival of a zooming fly mysteriously gets the job done.
ISBN 0-8037-1431-9—ISBN 0-8037-1432-7 (lib. bdg.)
[1. Cleanliness—Fiction. 2. Orderliness—Fiction.
3. Pets—Fiction.] I. Sneed, Brad, ill. II. Title.
PZ7.P44174Wh 1994 [E]—dc20 92-39807 CIP AC

The art for each picture is a watercolor painting,
scanner-separated and reproduced in full color.

For Nate
L.W.P.

For my grandparents,
Glenn and Eunice Johnson
and
Raymond Sneed
B.S.

In a quiet room a dreaming dog wagged his tail. A fuzzy cat snoozed. A plump hamster napped in a shoe. And a sleepy parakeet whistled on the bedpost.

"I can't clean my room," a child whispered to his mother. "All the animals are sleeping. I'll clean it later."

When a fly flew in, the dog opened an eye,
wiggled a whisker, then leaped up to catch it.

The fly turned left, and the dog's tail
sent a dozen dinosaurs sailing.

The fly turned right, and the dog's tail swept
off a mountain of muddy pants and crusty socks.

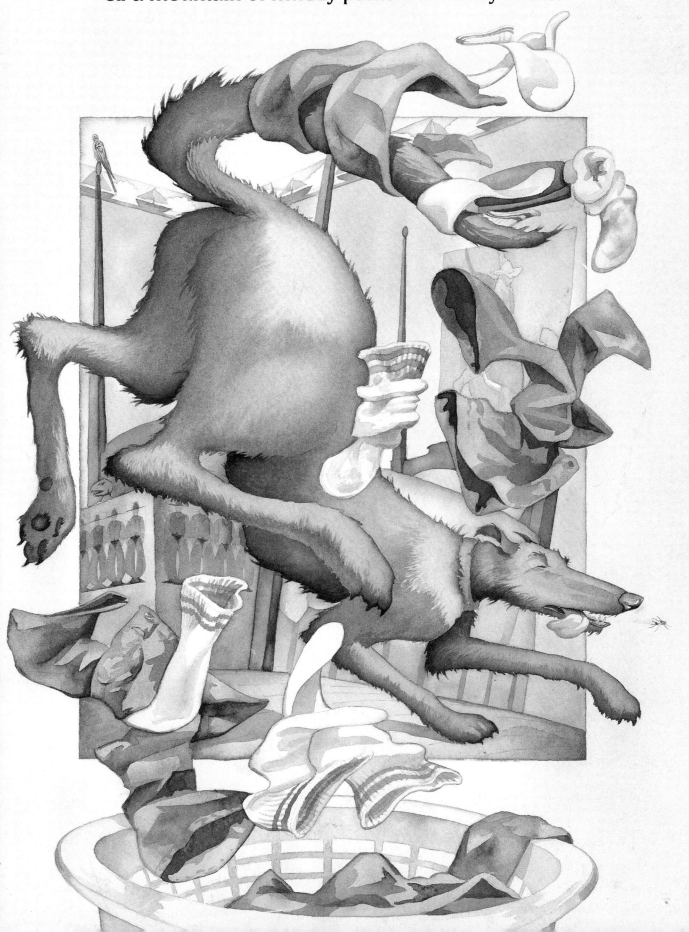

The fly turned in circles, and the dog's tail pushed off a pile of moldy old apple cores and banana peels. But the fly was always one turn ahead of the dog.

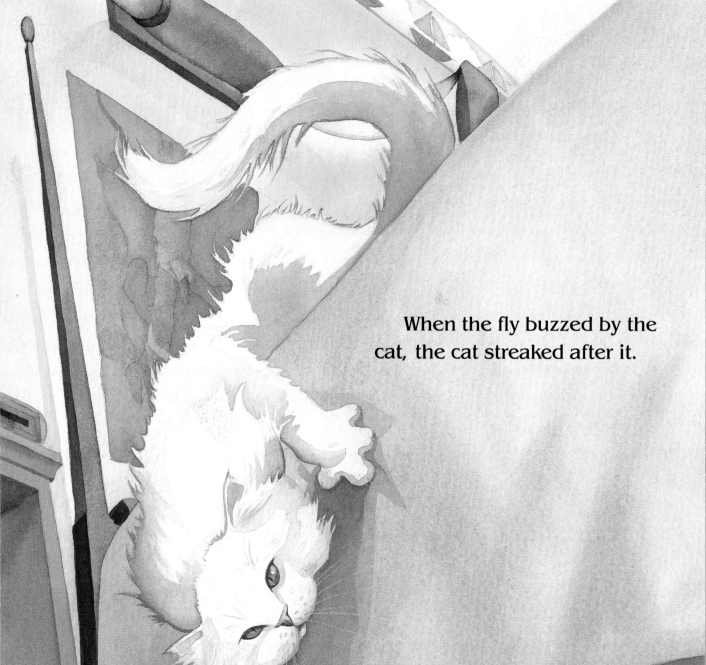

When the fly buzzed by the cat, the cat streaked after it.

The fly zigged. The cat zagged.

The fly zagged. The cat zigged.

But the fly was always a zig or a zag
ahead of the dust-mop cat.

When the fly stopped to nibble on a cookie crumb in the closet, the hamster took notice. The hamster didn't care about flies, but he did care about cookies.

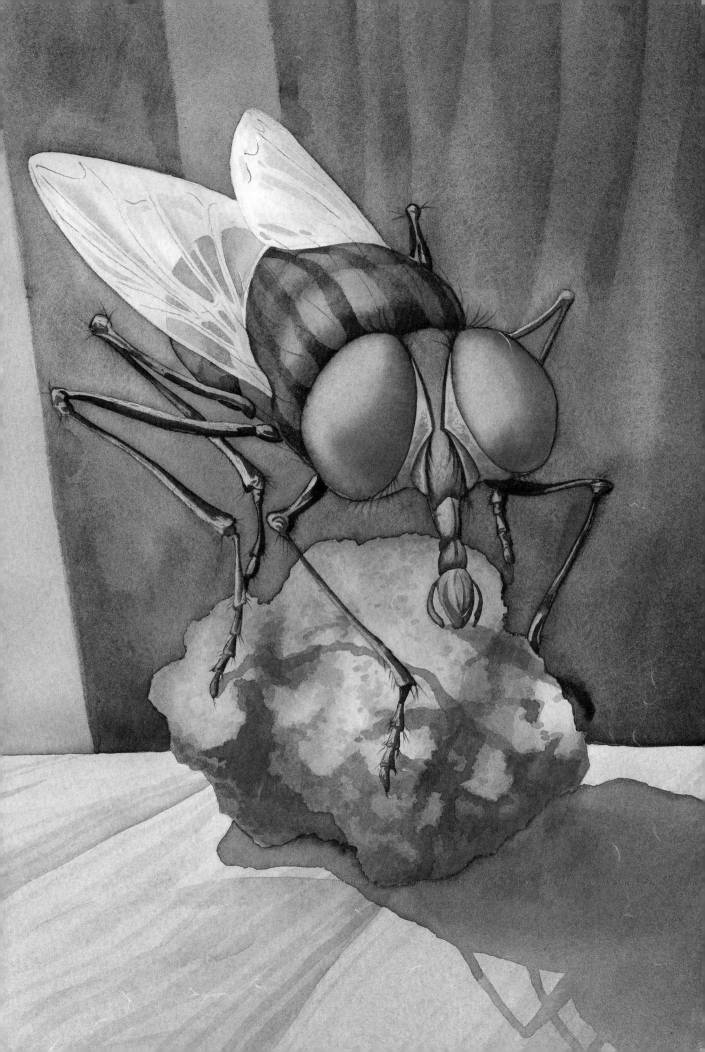

He shooed the fly away and ate the
crumb in the closet…

then the raisins on the radio…

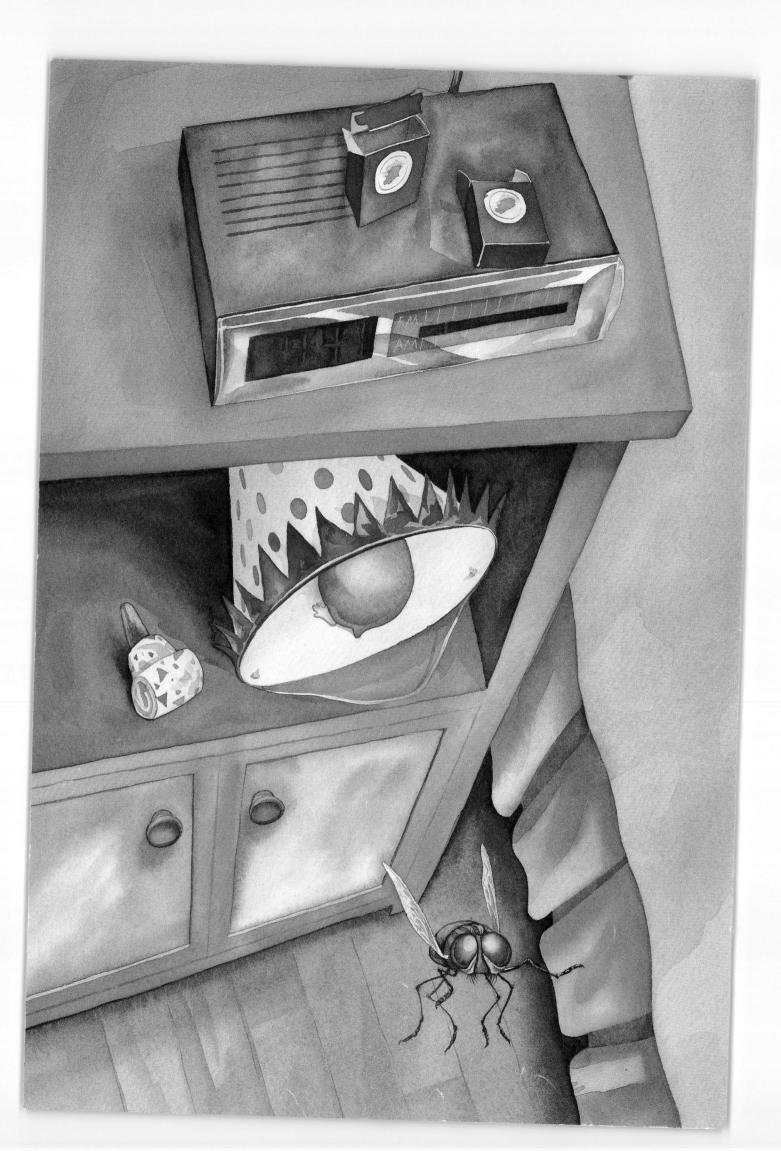

even the popcorn inside a party hat. But the fly
always stayed one nibble ahead of the hamster.

When the fly zipped around the ceiling, the parakeet watched closely because watching flies is a bird's business. But she couldn't watch any longer.

Zoom! She swooped into a corner full of cobwebs.

Zap! She flapped behind the curtains, thick
with more webs.

The parakeet gobbled up the spiders, and their webs trailed from her wings like kite strings.

But the fly was always one web ahead of her.

In a quiet room a dog twitched his tail as
he dreamed about flies. A cat curled up, her coat
licked clean.

A hamster settled down for a second nap. A weary
parakeet fluffed her feathers.

The fly flew out…

and the room was clean.